Mean Steam Riders

J. H. Williams

Illustrated By Millard Sexty

Mean Steam Riders

J. H. Williams

Published by John Hoover Williams, 2022.

MEAN STEAM RIDERS

First edition. October 3, 2022.

ISBN: 979-8231767120

Written by J. H. Williams.

Table of Contents

Epilogue
(Gale Forced)

THE COMMODORE KNEW something was amiss when he heard Chewy calling for him. It must be important he thought, because Chewy or in fact none of the humans ventured to the very bowels of the ship where he and his pack made their quarters unless something was up.

"Commodore, Commodore, wake your furry backside up you bloody rodent!" Chewy bellowed, popping his head through the lowest deck hatch. Small hammocks ran along to the bulkheads for the single guys and individual cabins for the families were amidships on beams to avoid the bilge water. Unlike human crews the rodents wouldn't think of traveling the seas without their families.

It was early 1845 and they were aboard a support steamship five days out from Japan where Admiral Perry had just completed a historic trade agreement with the isolated nation. Japan had closed its shores to foreign nations for centuries, but a fleet of heavily armed side-wheeled steamships proved to be the perfect diplomatic overture to convince the island nation to welcome world trade to their shores.

"Over here Chewy," the Commodore said. "Is something wrong?" he asked even though he knew there was. Things were getting rough, so he knew the seas were kicking up.

"Oh, there you are furball," said the red-faced cook. "Mighty storm ahead, you won't be safe down here. We'll be taking on some sea and the bilge will be filling up."

The rest of the ship's crew weren't as friendly as Chewy towards the seafaring rodents but over the years he and the Commodore had become close. The crew always gave Chewy a tough time about his grub since nothing he cooked was what you would call fork tender, hence the nickname. On the other hand, the Commodore always praised whatever Chewy rustled up which led to their friendship and provided some extra scraps for the below deck pack.

"Aya, Aye," said the Commodore. "Thank you Chewy we'll move to higher ground."

"Good then," said the cook as he scurried back to the galley to tighten things down.

"Storm stations, storm stations!" yelled the Commodore. "Pass the word storm stations!" "This is not a drill!" The pack knew what to do. This wasn't the first storm they'd been through, and it wouldn't be the last.

Quickly but efficiently, they prepared the move to a higher level. Down came the hammocks to be used to bundle clothes, pots, tools and anything else they couldn't afford to lose. It would be colder up top so on came the leather jackets made from scraps the crew discarded. Some things like straw mattresses could easily be remade when it was safe to return so they'd be left behind. Once the packing was done, they began the orderly evacuation to the lifeboats. The lifeboats had been chosen as their upper-level retreat because they were covered, stocked with emergency provisions and away from the human crew who wouldn't be thrilled to share their quarters. Half the pack went to starboard and the other half to the port side lifeboats. If something disastrous happened short of the whole ship going down, having two groups on opposite sides of the ship would ensure the pack lived on.

The storm blasted into the ship sooner than expected. Gale force winds and white caps were hitting the deck with thunderous force. Fortunately, the women and children had all made it through the small opening in the tarp before the worst of it hit. The Commodore stayed on deck watching his crew fight their way across a taut line to the opening one by one as the ship buckled back and forth. He wouldn't leave the storm washed deck until he was sure everyone else was safe inside. Once he heard the call "All onboard skipper," he too fought the wind and rain across the line into the opening of what he thought was their temporary shelter.

As his eyes adjusted to the dim light under the tarp, he could see the drills were paying off. Even though the boat was swaying much more than in the drills, all hands were doing their duties. Loose gear was being stowed, battened down and what little wash had made it in was being bailed.

"Well done everyone," said the Commodore. "This feels like a big one so secure yourselves with lifelines. We could be in for a rough ride." The words were hardly out of his mouth when they heard the loud CRACK! "Hang on!" he yelled as the bow of the lifeboat dropped straight down. "AAAHHHHHHH!" they all screamed. Their haven was now swinging like a bell above the choppy sea. The Commodore fought his way up to the back of the boat. Popping his head out of the tarp he could see that the forward pulley had broken loose which was bad enough on its own, but the worst was yet to come. As he looked above his head the lone rope they were hanging by, the last link to the Mothership was fraying from the swaying and was about to go. "BRACE!" he yelled "WE'RE GOING IN!"

When the line gave way time slowed down. Bracing for impact the Commodore watched the side of the ship glide by. It seemed like he could count every plank, every rivet as they dropped to the angry sea. When the bow hit it was as if they were cradled by the Pacific. Two thirds of the lifeboat plunged below the waterline, but the tarp kept most of the water out. They popped back to the surface like a cork and bounced with the waves as the as the ship steamed away leaving them behind, alone in the turbulent sea.

The stormed raged all night tossing and spinning the lifeboat in every direction. By morning it had passed leaving a calm sea and the pack to face their fate. No one was coming for them, and they had no propulsion. Over the years they had observed the ships crew and learned how to harness the power of steam but had no materials to build a boiler large enough to propel the lifeboat. Their destination would be determined by the currents. There was no panic, no fear, no fret, only a focus to survive. Hammocks were hung, family quarters built, a mess hall, workshops, rain catchers, a community re-established, prepared to survive however long it took to land ashore or find a new ship to board.

Not a single ship had been sighted since the night of the storm. The Commodore knew they must have been swept out of the shipping lanes so finding safe haven beyond the lifeboat would mean a landfall. Scooping plankton from the boats edge was supplementing the food rations and the tarp collected enough dew to provide fresh water so monotony was their only challenge. Fifty-seven lines etched on the inner hull marked the sunsets of their journey the night it came to an end.

"Land Ho!" shouted the night watch, "Land Ho!"

Scurrying up top the Commodore scanned the darkness of the moonless sea. "Where?" he asked as he could see no land.

"I'm not sure sir," responded the watchman, "I can't see it, but I can hear it!"

Motioning for silence the Commodore cupped his ear and smiled as he heard it too. The unmistakable sound of waves hitting shore. It wasn't long before the lifeboat picked up speed as the waves pushed it forward.

"Brace yourselves," warned the Commodore, "this could be rough."

It wasn't. The lifeboat rode the waves with ease and meet the beach with a gentle thud. Excitement flowed through them all as they packed up their gear and prepared to leave the vessel that had been home for almost two months. As the sun rose to light the beach they were overwhelmed by the beauty of their new home. The tide had pulled away through the night, leaving the lifeboat landlocked on the white sandy beach. Wasting no time, they packed up all they could carry and headed inland through the tree line to search for a place to shelter. Finding a clearing shaded by foliage they setup a camp.

Months became years, years became decades and decades turned to centuries. Generation after generation pulled together to establish a lasting colony built on community, trust and steam.

Chapter One
(Hit the Beach)

MAJOR PULLED THE TREADER to the top of the dune. Dead ahead was Blinder Beach where they would be collecting today. Appropriately named as on a clear day half an hour after sunrise the blazing rays reflecting off the clear blue waters were so intense you couldn't look into them. The treader's boiler was clanking and hissing as usual so he could barely hear Tinker complaining about Milo.

"He was supposed to meet us here," she said. "We should know better to let him head off on his own."

Deuce had been behind them the whole way and pulled his steam cycle up next to them. "Where's Milo?" he said. "He should have beat" but before he could get the "us here" out Milo's screamer steamer came flying over the dune.

"MEAN STEAM!" Screamed Milo as he streaked by them completely airborne. His descent was less graceful though as he came to earth with a "WHOMP" forcing a safety release of steam out of the boiler as Tinker had designed. Coming back around he slowly pulled his weakened steamer up even with the guys and said meekly with a sheepish grin "lean steam."

"Someday," said Tinker "Milo someday Uno's going to catch you with a lean boiler and all we'll find is your cap and goggles."

Uno is a one-eyed massive Sea Eagle that for some reason had it out for Milo and his crew. So far, his lack of depth perception had allowed for some narrow escapes.

"Hadn't got me yet," yelled a cocky Milo. "Come on Deuce my steams back up let's practice making Uno miss." Milo and Deuce took off over the dunes practicing evasive maneuvers while Tinker and Major sat back out of the way. The tracker could pull huge loads, but it was not made to fly the dunes in fact Tinker didn't think any of the steam machines were.

"Take it easy on my machines," she yelled. "I made them for collecting, not for banging over dunes."

Milo didn't hear her as he was already flying over the first dune. He shot straight up the dune but transitioned into a zig zag coming down the other side. Uno attacks at blistering speed diving straight in from above but side to side movement gave him problems so staying low to the ground in a serpentine pattern was the key to dodging his attacks.

Out of the corner of his eye Milo spotted Deuce flying over the crest grabbing some major air. "Oh, he'll pluck you right out of the air if you do that Deuce," he yelled. "You gotta stay on the ground in a constant zig zag. Once you leave the ground you can't maneuver."

"Easy for you to say Milo you've got four wheels," Deuce yelled back. "This baby will fly through the sand going dead on but back and forth is a chore, but I get your point so let's boogie some."

They shot up the next dune side by side cutting left and right as they climbed. They crested the top turning into a right-angle zig but as they steered to a left side zag the rear tire of Deuce's cycle hit an empty pocket of sand sinking the rear end and killing his momentum. Seeing he no longer had a dancing partner Milo fishtailed around to see if Deuce was all right.

"Bogged it," they both said laughing together as Deuce worked his tire back to full sand.

Milo, Tinker, Major and Deuce are collectors. They search the beaches of the tiny pacific island for anything the pack can use to keep the village safe and comfortable. Pieces of net, driftwood, bottles, metal canisters, moss, seaweed and rope all wash ashore on a daily basis and it's their job to collect the good stuff and get it back to the village. Unfortunately, more plastic bottles than anything else are washing ashore these days and they're not good for much.

The pack are all descendants of the twenty-nine founders. The group of sea-going rats washed overboard from a steamship in the mid 1800's. Fortunes were with them as waves pushed them upon this tiny uncharted island where they found enough food, water and shelter to establish a colony that still thrives today. Steam powered the world then and almost two centuries later on this tiny spec in the Pacific Ocean it still does.

Tinker is the Master of the boilers, as was her father before her and his father before him and his father before him through the centuries back to the founders. She's mechanically brilliant and has engineered the colony's use of steam energy far beyond where it was before her. Officially she's not one of the collectors but likes to come along in case of breakdowns. Steam can be a fickle source of power especially with Milo's heavy hand. She also likes to help in the search for any washed-up materials that can be transformed into a steam machine.

Major is the hauler. He can get his steam truck and trailer in and out of anywhere no matter how heavy the load. He will push the limits but that's what he does best, stack, organize and manage the weight. When he says no more it means no more. He's the oldest and is like a big brother to the others. His age should have him in charge, but he would rather manage the load than the crew.

Deuce is the scout. He'll recon ahead of the rest on his steam chopper to scope out possibilities. If there's not much to grab, they'll head to another beach.

And then there's Milo, pure energy living life on the edge. If it wasn't for the other three, he probably would have gone over it by now. His motto is if you have to think it through it takes too long.

He's quick on his feet and even faster on wheels. Without Tinker making constant repairs to his steamer, it would have been scrap by now.

"All present and accounted for" he bellowed. "Let's hit the beach and earn our keeps."

Chapter Two
(Meeting Albert Ross)

HEADING OVER THE DUNES and onto the beach the team fell into standard formation. Deuce takes the lead and will pull ahead to scout around; Milo follows him in the screamer and Major's heavy plodding treader and trailer take up the rear. But this day things would take a turn. Normally Deuce would have immediately sprung far out onto the beach but today he pulled up and waited for the others to catch up.

"What's that?" he said, pointing to a large mound up the beach.

"I don't know," Milo replied. "Let's go check it out." They headed towards the mystery mass and as they approached it became clear that tangled in a fishing net and draped in seaweed was what at one time had been a very large bird.

As they approached the trussed up fowl they were startled by the voice of an uninvited pest.

"Oh what have we here", said a creepy voice behind them.

Spinning around they could see Sleazel the Weasel, behind them rubbing his hands, licking his lips and looking as devious as ever.

"Beat it Sleazball," said Milo brandishing his work knife like a weapon. "We don't need your help!"

"But it's so big", claimed the Weasel, it will feed all of us for days!"

"We don't eat birds and you know that," responded an irritated Milo, and if your boss pal Uno heard you talking like that he won't like it."

"Now, now, said the Weasel, "We wouldn't have to tell him would we. You scratch my tummy and I'll scratch yours and they can all be full of this giant beach bird once we eat it."

The mention of a bird being eaten must have hit a nerve as a huge eyeball within the net popped open right in front of where they were standing.

"AAAAAAHHHHHHHHHHHHHHHHHH!" they all screamed including the supposedly dead bird. The weasel high tailed it without looking back as the others scrambled behind rocks and beach trash. They all peeked back at the trussed-up fowl. It wasn't moving towards them, in fact it probably couldn't so Milo came out from behind the rock and slowly walked towards it.

"What are you doing Milo, that thing could eat you," said a nervous Tinker.

"It needs our help Tinker. We can't just leave it like that." "You won't eat us if we help you out of this mess, will you?" Asked Milo as he approached the open eyeball.

"Probably not," said the bird, "I mostly eat fish."

"That wasn't a no!" Tinker pointed out," probably not isn't no I would never."

"Hush," said Milo as he introduced them. "I'm Milo and this is Tinker, Deuce and Major. We collect things off the beach."

"Pleasure to meet cha Milo. I am Albert Ross." said the bird. "Will you be collecting me?"

"Albert Ross?" questioned Tinker. "That's not who you are, that's what you are. You're an Albatross."

Looking back at Tinker with a bit of disdain Albert said with conviction, "What you are is who you are, and I are Albert Ross."

"Pleasure to meet you Albert Ross," said Milo. "No, we won't be collecting you but we could use that net you're wrapped in. Looks like you're stuck so we'll be happy to cut you out of there."

"Does it?" Albert Ross answered. "I don't know, I figure eventually I'll be able to squiggle out of this. You know there is something tremendously calming about not being able to move. No decisions to make, schedules to meet, no hustle, no bustle, just complete and total stillness."

"Well, that inner peace could turn to inner pieces when the evening crabs come out and size you up as a carcass for the taking, but if you want us to leave you alone to your motionless meditations we'll be on our way." Milo quipped.

"No, I think I'll take you up on the assistance," exclaimed the big bird. "As much as I'd love to spend the rest of my life lounging on the beach, if it's only going to be a few more hours the appeal is somewhat diminished. I would be grateful to accept your offer of assistance. By all means unwrap these bonds of serenity."

So the boys set to work to free the Albert's bonds. It wasn't a speedy job, feathers, seaweed, net and limbs were all tangled in one huge mass. Every cut measured to limit damage to his feathers. Leaving the bird flightless with clipped wings would defeat the purpose of freeing him but his jerking and twitching wasn't making the job any easier.

"Tickles, tickles, eeewww yahhh tickles," he giggled.

"This would go a lot quicker if you'd stay still," Milo told him. "We're trying to be careful but you're not helping any."

"Tickles," Albert Ross whispered.

Seemed like forever but they were finally done. Deuce had no sooner cut the last bit of net when the big bird sprang to his feet, spread   his   wings   and   let   out   a   gratifying "AAAAAAAAHHHHHHHH! Oh this feels great!" he said as he stretched his wings further and further. "AAAAAAHHHHHHHH OH OH OH OH Oooouch!" he shouted. "Cramp, cramp, cramp, cramp!" He said in pain as he tried to walk it off. "Golly stretching feels so good until it doesn't."

"Thank you, gentlemen, and er lady, your assistance is much appreciated. I owe you one or four as it would seem. In the future if you find yourself in need, I most surely won't be around but if I am I will be pleased and obligated to repay your kindness."

"Does this guy ever shut up" Tinker whispered to Milo.

"Hush," said Milo. "Sounds like you're not planning on staying long." He said to the still stretching fowl.

"No," said Albert Ross. "I am a wandering soul, a vagabond, drifter of the skies, a fly-by-night who flies by day. My life is a constant journey guided by the winds. Literally in this case, as a very big storm blew me horrendously off course, lost above an empty pounding sea until fortune roughly deposited me into the shallow shores of your island haven. Unfortunately, it had also deposited a fair amount of sea going debris which as you witnessed made my debut to your sandy beaches somewhat tangled."

"It'll be dark soon so we need to set up camp for the night. You're welcome to share our fire." Invited Milo.

"Thank you." The big bird replied. "Relaxing by a warm fire, staring at the stars, swapping stories with collectors of the beach and saviors of the bound sounds like a wonderful way to spend the evening. I'd loved to join you.

After packing the net that once contained Albert into Major's truck the group scooped up somedry wood for the nights fire and found a comfy spot on the beach to pass the night.

Chapter Three
(Who Are Us)

AS THE SUN FADED BEHIND the hills the stars came to light the steam driven collectors and wayward Albatross settle in for a restful evening. Tinker is checking and tweaking the steamers as she always does when down time presents itself. Major and Deuce were focused on a game of checkers they rigged up with shells and stones on a sand drawn board. Milo and Albert Ross sit comfortably beside the warming fire Tinker had stoked with an ember from the truck's boiler.

Albert Ross propped his feet up on a rock, leaned back and put his wings behind his head. "You know Milo I haven't seen much of your little island here but I'm liking what I have seen, sandy beaches, warm water, brilliant sunsets and star filled night skies. If I had to define comfort and serene this would be it."

"Yeah," Milo responded. "We have a lot of that but it's not always like this. The storm you got caught up in hit us pretty hard. The town's torn up a bit so we need to collect materials to repair some roofs and fences. We also have Uno to contend with. It's not so calm and serene around here when he drops in."

"Uno?" "What's an Uno?" asked Albert Ross.

"No, it's your turn, big bird, what's your story?" Milo inquired. "What's it like where you're from?"

"I don't really have a from," Albert answered. "As long as I can remember I've been on the move, place to place, on the road again or I guess more like in the air again. You might say this ocean and its shores are my home. Oh, and the ships too, thank goodness for the ships out there, I was hatched on one. Nothing better than spotting a big old cargo ship when the wings are tired. Those things are pretty much islands with propellers, and I feel more at home there than on dry land. They stack big metal boxes on top of each other way, way high so you can just land on top of those things and cruise the sea. They're great for resting the old wing muscles. They may not take you where you're going but they'll move you from where you are. You find them in these things called shipping lanes and if you navigate around them there will always be a huge diesel driven rest stop passing by soon enough."

"Diesel driven?" Milo asked with a confused look. "Not steam?"

"No, never seen a steam driven ship", Albert replied. "Though it might smell better."

"I thought everything was steam driven." Milo added.

"No, don't think so", answered Albert. That's what makes life fun though, learning new things. There was a time that I thought this corner of the Pacific was the whole enchilada and I had seen all there was to see but a little shipboard eavesdropping made me realize that the world's a much bigger place. Do you know there's more than one ocean? From what I've overheard sailors say on those ships there are lots of oceans and seas and huge chunks of land called continents. Makes Albert Ross feel kind of small."

"Well from where I sit you're not small at all," Milo said with a smile.

"So anywho that's what I was doing the day destiny brought me here." Albert continued. "Sitting back like you see me now on top of a cargo stack soaking in some sun when the loudest thing I've ever heard about turned me inside out. BBBOOOOONNNNKKKKKK, BBBOOOOONNNNKKK, BBBOOOOONNNNKKK came blaring out of nowhere followed by ALERT! ALERT! ALERT! INCLEMENT WEATHER APPROACHING, SECURE ALL HATCHES, BATTEN DOWN

ALL LOOSE OBJECTS! THIS IS NOT A DRILL! I'd never be so awake in my life and when I settled down and got my heart back in rhythm, I could see that it was indeed not a drill."

"Sounds like it's about to get exciting," Milo piped in.

"If terror excites you then yes exciting it was," Albert said as he continued. "The sun faded to darkness as the wind began to blow and the relaxing upper level penthouse I was perched on became increasingly unstable as the ship plowed on into rougher and rougher seas. It was clearly time to make my exit so I took flight away from the storm hoping I could stay ahead of its path which as you have probably surmised was false hope indeed. I had never flapped so hard in my life as I raced the wind and rain to no avail. The pelting rain was making it harder and harder to keep my wings in motion and the gusts were so strong I realized that I was no longer in flight but instead had become a projectile in motion going only where the wind allowed."

"Then what happened?" asked Tinker, who had been drawn into Alberts tale.

"Gets a little blurry after that," Albert concluded. "Tucked in a ball, blowing, blowing, blowing, hit the water, hit the sand, hit some net thingy, tangled, exhausted, sleeping so sound until I heard you guys plotting to eat me."

"That wasn't us that was Sleazel the Weasel", clarified Milo. "He's always popping up out of nowhere to muddy the waters. He's the only Lucky for us all he's the only Weasel on the island. We would never have eaten you though if you hadn't opened your eyes we may have plucked a few feathers.

"Thank you, very reassuring," replied Albert. "Back to you now, I've been blabbering. Give me a little Milo and the beach cleaners history lesson and don't forget the Uno part."

"Well, we were born and raised on this island and have never considered going anywhere else so guess you can say this is our world," Milo explained. "Over a hundred years ago our ancestors traveled the seas like you on a big steamship but also like you a huge storm blew them overboard and onto this island so in a roundabout way we all ended up here in much the same way."

"Isn't that something!" Albert declared.

"As you know we come to the dunes and beaches to gather everything that's useful. We grab all the best and leave the rest." Milo bragged. "Our village is inland tucked between the hills where the founders built the first huts. It's protected by the hills and thick tropical foliage so it's very peaceful and safe. Not even Uno bothers us there."

"Ah yes let's not forget about Uno," quipped Albert.

"Well," said Milo, "Uno is the biggest, nastiest, smelliest one-eyed Sea Eagle you've ever seen, and he really seems to hate us, me in particular. He only bothers us when we're picking the beaches and dunes but fortunately his depth perception is limited so we've managed to avoid his massive claws. If he wasn't single sighted, he'd be tougher to avoid. He uses the Weasel as his little spy to slink around and snoop. The Weasel just washed up one day from a neighboring island that's supposedly full of them. We don't know if he got washed to sea or they kicked him off but unfortunately for us he's one of us now. Hopefully you'll never cross paths with Uno or if you do, he doesn't take to hating you like he does us."

"I'll keep that in mind," Albert said as he yawned. "Probably won't be here too long as tomorrow I'll be scanning the horizon for my next free ride to nowhere."

As the fire began to fade, they all settled in for a full night's sleep comforted by the warm tropical breeze and soothing symphony of the breaking ocean waves.

As they drifted off a slinking sinister shadow crept from behind a nearby dune. Scampering along the water's edge the meddlesome Weasel hurried to find and report in to the giant Eagle.

Chapter Four
(Milo Takes Off)

ALBERT ROSS WAS ENGULFED by the silence, energized by the purity of the clean crisp air and overwhelmed at the beauty of the world far below. He was reaching for the stars at the gates of heaven as he flew higher than any bird had ever attempted. High above the hustle of the blue planet below he was inspired by the serenity, invigorated by the ease in which he had reached such heights and thoroughly confused that someone was calling his name. "Albert, hey Albert."

"Morning Albert, sorry if we woke you up," said Milo. "We like to get the boilers hot before sunrise so we can hit the beach at the break of dawn. You're welcome to join us if you'd like."

Albert looked around with sleepy eyes to see Milo putting the still glowing embers from the night's fire into a metal bucket as the pack worked in unison to prepare for the day. Deuce was packing and stowing gear as Tinker and Major worked on the boilers. Tinker was putting the hot embers into the fireboxes while Major filled the tanks with water. A full tank could feed the boiler all day if they didn't push it too hard.

"Thanks Milo, I appreciate the invite, but I think I'll just search the shallows for some breakfast and keep an eye on the horizon for another free ride to wherever," Albert said as he yawned and stretched. "I sure do thank you all for freeing me from my beached bound predicament. I am forever in your debt, and I do probably mean forever as my wandering nomadic ways may never bring me back to repay the kindness you are due."

"Geez," whispered Tinker. "This guy takes a week to say goodbye."

"No worries Big Guy," added Milo. "We're glad we came along when we did. If you ever decide you want to settle down, you'll certainly be welcome here. C'mon guys let's hit the beach," he yelled as he pulled away from camp waving at Albert on the way out. Albert waved back at the rat packs mean steam machines as they bounced and hissed across the dunes making their way to the dawn lit beach. "That's a scrappy bunch of rodents," he thought to himself as his mind started to slowly focus on the breakfast he may find along the water's edge. "Don't mind if I do," he said to himself as he popped up, shook off the sand and headed to the beach.

As the morning sun brightened the beach Albert waded through the warm clear water looking for the slight cup of sand air bubble that may give away the lair of a hidden morsel. Being hungry and focused on breakfast he paid no attention to the shadow circling his position nor the muffled sound of flapping wings and the breeze they stirred on his back. He eagerly approached his first bit of breakfast but before making his move he was startled by a deep booming voice from behind.

"Hey Tross!" he heard which made him jump and spin quickly around. In front of him stood a huge, scruffy, mean looking Sea Eagle with a patch over one eye and a not so welcoming look on his face.

"Well hello," said Albert, "that would be Ross, Albert Ross. You must be..."

"Don't matter who I am," interrupted the menacing intruder, "I know what you are, but I don't know who you are? We don't get many strangers around here and we like it that way."

"Well, I'm just passing through," said Albert. "Blown in by the storm but now that things have calmed down, I'll be heading along once I catch sight of a seagoing taxi."

"See that you do," barked the Eagle. "Word is you've been hanging out with the worst of the worst around here which won't be good for you if you keep it up."

"Oh no not at all," Albert replied. "I haven't had time to meet anybody except a great bunch of young rats that saved me from an awkward predicament I found myself in after my windblown arrival. Yep, Milo and the gang are the only..."

"MILO IS WHO I'M TALKING ABOUT!" bellowed the obviously irritated fowl. "That smart aleck rat and his criminal crew are the biggest bunch of thieves on the island and I'm going to put a stop to it. Once I get my talons into that scrawny rat he'll wish he had never been born. If you know what's good for you you'll forget you ever met him cause after I deal with him I'll deal with his accomplices! Get my drift Tross?"

"It's Ross, and yes your drift has been received but rest assured once I have downed a nice breakfast and acquired a suitable platform of extraction I will be on my way," Albert responded.

"See that you are," The Eagle shot back as he took flight with one swift swipe of his wings.

"Though I must say," Albert shouted up at him as he flew away. "I think you have Milo and his crew all wrong." "Grumpy son of a gun," he mused as his attention once again returned to breakfast. "Wish I could take off like that," he thought before once again having his morning chow interrupted.

"You better listen to him buddy boy or this could be your last meal", the sneaky Weasel suggested as he popped up from seemingly nowhere.

"Oh it's you," a hungry and perturbed Albert responded. You're Sleazel or something like that aren't you?"

"I am Slaysall," shot back the irritated Weasel. "Descendant of Slaysall the Conqueror, slayer of many and ruler of all."

"Never heard of em," Albert quipped. "But I'm sure he was a great guy. Now if you don't mind or frankly even if you do I'm going to find me some breakfast."

Turning back towards the water's edge Albert suddenly remembered that this same creepy Weasel was thinking of having him for breakfast yesterday so he spun back around to find him slowly creeping up from behind."

"You thinking what I think you're thinking Sleazball," Albert barked out at the shocked Weasel. "I may not have the talons of your big boss bird but I've got a beak that can pound you into putty," he threatened.

"Oh no Mister Bird I wasn't thinking what you think I was thinking, at least I don't think I was thinking that," a suddenly meek and somewhat confused Sleazel answered. "I was just thinking that it's time for me to go," he yelped while turning to scamper back off the beach as quick as he could.

Albert kept an eye on him until he was out of sight before turning back to the shallows, "Milo sure was right about that guy. I wouldn't trust him as far as I could spit him," he thought to himself as he once again focused back on some morning chow.

Further up the coast the boys were crossing the dunes towards today's beach of choice. Tinker and Major chugged along in the Treader side by side with Milo's Mean Steamer as Deuce took the lead.

"Hey Milo," Tinker yelled. "Don't forget I brought the sky screamer for a test flight today."

"We'll see," Milo yelled back. "We didn't get anything done yesterday so we need to focus on getting loaded up. If we have any light left when we're done we can play with your new toy." Milo wasn't as thrilled as Tinker about her latest attempt to send him skyward. Tinker had been bragging for years that she was on the verge of perfecting a steam powered flying machine but so far, every test had been a bust so Milo had little enthusiasm for the project. As far as he was concerned the only flying he'd ever do would be screaming off the top of a dune.

As they crested to the beach, they could see it was going to be a busy day. The storm had deposited twice the debris they would normally deal with which was good and bad. Good because the village would have plenty of material to work with for the repairs and bad because the steam machines would be loaded to the max making the trek home slow and risky. If Uno decided to show up there would be no way to outrun him with the load they'd be carrying. Even Deuce would need to pack a load on the steam cycle.

"Okay guys, busy day ahead. Let's get to it," Milo shouted out. With that the crew hit the beach in standard formation. Tinker and Major positioned the tracker and trailer to sweep the top half of the beach towards the dunes while Milo and Deuce took the bottom section towards the water's edge. No one had to be told what to do, once they started sweeping that's all they focused on. When the work started all thoughts of dune jumping, donut making, or new craft testing were stowed until later. There was plenty to pick today so they got to it.

Anything useful that could fit in the vehicles would be collected and stacked. Major had a hand winch he could mount on the trackers side, so he grabbed the heavier pieces while everyone else collected by hand. Deuce hooked and dragged the clear pliable bottles to get them out of the way. More and more of them have been showing up but since they weren't good for much, he just neatly stacked them out of the way.

They were after the good stuff, wood, twine, metal bits, pieces of net and even the stringy seaweed that could be dried into a strong binding material. The clear bottles could be cut up to use for roofing or walls, but it was very noisy in the wind and no one really wanted clear walls so it was very low on the priority list of building materials.

Thanks to the storm there was plenty of the good stuff on hand and picking was good.

With so much to do, five hours flew by. "Let's break for lunch and mark our progress," Milo yelled to the crew, so they pulled together where he was positioned to take stock and fill their guts. While chowing down on coconut cheese Milo could see they were in good shape. Most of the beach was cleared but they still had some room, so he was pretty sure they'd get the whole thing cleared. Major and Tinker had the trailer stacked full but still had room in the trackers bed. Milo's steamer was pretty much packed, but Deuce had so many bottles to move nothing had been loaded onto the back of the steamer cycle yet. "Well Tinker," said Milo, "if we keep this up we may have a little time to test your new gizmo."

Tinker smiled back at him as best she could with both cheeks full of coconut cheese. "You're gunna ruv it," she said as bits of cheese flew out of her mouth.

After lunch they got back to work and steadily finished the task. Every once in a while one of them would catch a glimpse of a weaselly figure lurking around in the distance but paid it no mind. They knew he was always out there so why waste any time worrying about it.

Major and Deuce started topping off the boilers with water for the haul back to the village. Since they had to wait for the steam to build back up Milo figured he'd let Tinker tinker. She was a genius at designing land steamers but every flying contraption she had ever come up with was a complete and utter failure so he knew it probably wouldn't take much time.

"Okay Tinker," he said. "Let's give your new Tinker Sinker a whirl." Tinker hadn't waited for Milo's go ahead. She was already enthusiastically monkeying with the gizmo.

"I think I've got it this time Milo I really do," she said with excitement. "The problem in the past was the steam. Boilers, fireboxes and steam engines are just too heavy to get off the ground.

So now taa daa," she exclaimed with elation as she motioned to her creation. "The Steam-less Air Streamer!" Next to her was a metal cylinder that tapered on the bottom with knobs, pull cords and straps. Big letters on the side said CO2 and tucked behind each side of the straps was something that looked like an accordion.

"Don't get it," said Milo. How is that going to fly with no steam to power it and no wings to float on?"

"It's got wings," Tinker answered. "They're folded up here on each side and should pop out when you pull this cord on the right."

"Should?" Milo questioned with concern.

"Well obviously they haven't been flight tested yet," Tinker answered. "Don't worry about them though because we shouldn't need them today. This first test is just to see if we can get off the ground. The cord on the left is for the parachute on the back. It should, ahhh I mean it will gently float you safely to the ground."

"Should huh," said a skeptical Milo. "Not too concerned though as I have a feeling I won't be leaving the ground."

"As for the power," Tinker continued. "It's just air! "I took one of those empty CO-two bottles that float in from time to time and filled it with air. Lots and lots of air packed in real tight so when we open the release valve, presto instant power!"

"If you say so," Milo said, jumping to his feet. "Let's get this over with so we can head home."

"Absolutely," said an excited Tinker. "Just strap this on to your back and make sure it's on tight. Now remember DON'T pull the cord on the right. That will release the wings which are still experimental. I made them out of those clear bottles so I'm not sure if they'll hold up."

"Got it, no wings," Milo repeated.

"The cord on the left will release the parachute and float you back down," Tinker continued. "This knob controls the release valve. As you turn it the packed air will come out of the bottom and propel you skyward. Just go easy with it as I don't know how much thrust you're going to have."

Milo strapped the contraption to his back with Tinker's help. "How's it feel?" Tinker asked as she tightened the straps. "Think you'll stay in it?"

"Yeah, I think I'll stay in it," Milo replied sarcastically as he reached for the release knob.

"Remember go easy," ordered Tinker as a doubtful Milo grabbed the knob and cranked it open. WHHHOOOOOSSHHHHHH was all Tinker heard as she watched Milo rocket skyward faster and higher than any steampunk rat had ever flown.

AAAAAAAAAAAAAHHHHHHHHHHHHHhhhh! Was all they heard until it tapered to silence.

"HOLY COCONUTS!" yelled Major.

Deuce was silent, amazed at the velocity pushing Milo higher and higher while Tinker jumped for joy at her success. "IT WORKED, IT WORKED, IT WORKED," she yelled with pride.

Milo on the other hand wasn't as thrilled. He had quit screaming about halfway up and was trying to make sense of it all. Far below he could see the guys getting smaller and smaller. As his speed started to slow it dawned on him that his flight was almost over and would soon become a descent. He was trying to recall the instructions from Tinker he thought he would never need when the last thing he could ever expect happened. He hit something.

"What the?" he thought to himself. As his ascent came to an end in what seemed like slow motion he looked down a few feet to see a startled one-eyed Sea Eagle flapping backwards and staring angrily at him.

"Hey Uno", Milo said with a sheepish grin as he began to fall back to earth.

"MILOOOOOOOOOOOOOOO," is all he heard from the bird as his downward decent picked up speed!

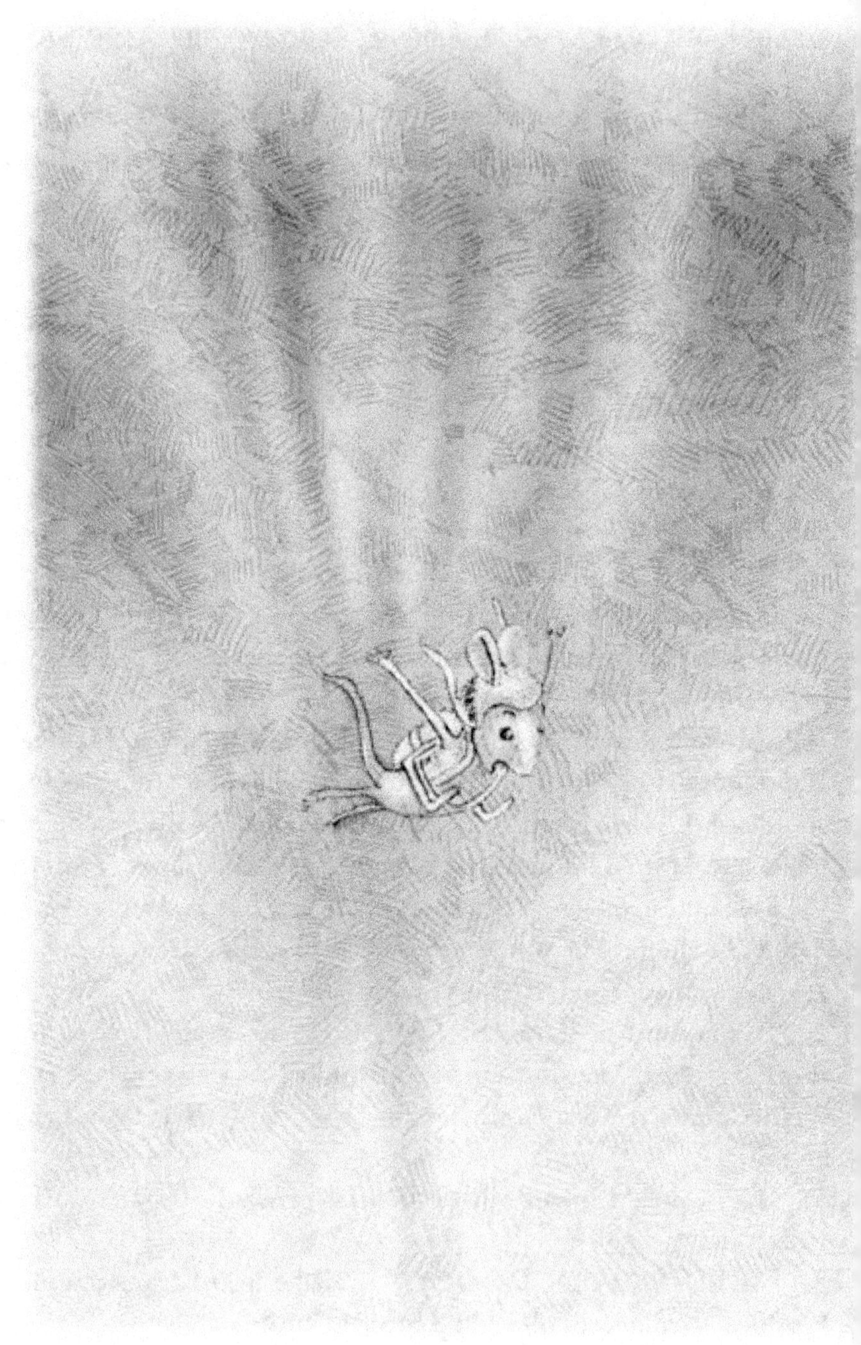

Chapter Five
(Milo Comes Down)

BELOW ON THE BEACH Deuce and Major followed Milo's flight while Tinker still danced with glee. "IT WORKED," she shouted for what seemed like the hundredth time.

"Looks like he hit something," said Major. "I think he's heading back now."

"IT WOR, wait what" responded a confused and suddenly concerned Tinker. "Hit something? What could he hit?" Looking up she shaded her eyes from the sun trying to make out what was happening. Milo was really up there but Tinker could see enough to grasp what had happened. "He hit a bird" she said, "he hit a big bird, AHH GEEZ he hit the biggest bird, HE HIT UNO!" Suddenly realizing Milo was in danger of crashing back to Earth or even worse coming down in Uno's claws she started screaming up at him. "PULL THE CHUTE, PULL THE CHUTE!"

"He may want to come down a bit before he does that," injected Major. "He opens that chute now he'll be a floating duck for old Uno up there."

"DON'T PULL THE CHUTE, DON'T PULL THE CHUTE," yelled a frazzled Tinker.

Milo was too caught up in his situation to care about what was going on below. For what seemed like forever he was floating a foot from a very angry Uno before the invisible trap door opened under his feet sending him and the empty canister strapped to his back plummeting back to ground at what seemed like the speed of light. It took Uno a second or two to come to terms with what had just happened but once he realized he had that pesky rat Milo defenseless in his domain he sprang into action.

Milo's arms and legs were flailing as if he could climb the air while his brain frantically tried to remember Tinker's instructions. "Wings, chute, cord, handle, left, right all rushed through his mind as he saw Uno out of the corner of his eye starting to dive. The two cords that had been calmly hanging below his chest on the way up were now being blasted by the windy pull of descent, battering his chin like a speed bag. Knowing he had to do something Milo grabbed the first cord handle he could get a hold of and yanked with all the strength he had left. WHACK he heard as the pair of clear wings made from beach bottles popped from each side of his back slowing his fall while sending him into a tight spiral glide. Uno pulled in inches behind.

"Got you now," he growled as they both rode currents of air in a circular plunge towards the ground below.

"They're coming down further up the beach," a worried Tinker exclaimed. "We have to get there before they come down to save Milo from Uno." Jumping into Milo's steamer Tinker led the crew towards the descending duo. Major and the heavily laden tracker couldn't keep up as Tinker in the steamer and Deuce on the steam cycle raced forward side by side. "Deuce do whatever you can to distract Uno while I grab Milo," yelled Tinker. "Spin sand in his face, roll his toes or even ram him if you have to, just give me time to grab Milo!"

"Will do," Deuce yelled back as he crouched lower on the bike. "Bird won't know what hit him," he thought to himself.

High above but lower every second Milo and Uno were locked in a circular descent. Milo thought of trying to pull out of it to level off and glide in for a soft landing but wasn't sure if the wings could take the strain and even if they could Uno would be on him in no time. Staying in the spiral was his only hope of keeping ahead of the angry bird but Milo could sense he was gaining on him. Only inches separated the two as Uno focused in on his kill shot. All he needed was a good chomp on that tail. If he could secure the tail the body would follow, and that tail was whipping back and forth right in front of his beak. He brought his wings in tight, angling them like a jet fighter to gain the little extra speed needed to make the strike. The ground was coming up fast, so it was now or never.

Milo knew it was time to act. He could feel Uno's breath on his tail and knew the beach was coming up fast. The spinning glide down had him dizzy and confused but with what little sense he had left he found the other pull cord and yanked. The chute popped open with such force he felt his organs shift. "What the!" he heard a befuddled Uno yell below him.

Uno had made his move. Feeling his momentum pulling him towards the middle of Milo's tail he took aim and chomped right where it had just been. Confused, mad and somewhat dizzy himself he looked up to see Milo and his chute slowly floating away above. Milo had his hands cupped over his mouth and Uno could barely hear him shouting, "pull up, pull up Uno!" "Pull what up?" he thought to himself as he hit the soft sandy beach tumbling beak over tailfeathers until coming to a stop rump up in the warm sand. As he floated back to Earth Milo could see Tinker and Deuce racing down the beach to rescue him but as he hit the sand his only concern was making sure Uno was okay.

Tinker raced up to Milo as he hit the ground, jumped from the steamer and slapped him on the back. "I told you it would work, I told you it would work," she bragged while helping Milo out of the harness. "You my friend are the first rat to fly!"

Milo was in a daze as he watched Deuce fly by and head over to Uno's crash site. Deuce spun the cycle in the beach near Uno's head and started spinning sand from the back tire onto Uno's head.

"STOP!" yelled Milo, "He might be hurt or even worse I might have killed him!" he said with distress. As Tinker loaded the empty rat rocket and chute on the back of the steamer Milo ran over to Deuce and the big, battered bird. "Uno are you okay?" he said with concern. Uno raised his head slowly shedding the sand Deuce had just piled on him. Somewhat wobbly he stared down at Milo and slowly gathered his senses.

"Yes I'm okay in fact I am so okay I'm GOING TO GET YOU MILO IF IT'S THE LAST THING I DO!" he bellowed as he popped to his feet spreading his wings in anger as he glared down at Milo. "Eww dizzy" he said before falling over onto his back with his feet in the air. "When everything stops spinning, I will get you."

"Looks okay to me," Tinker pointed out as she grabbed Milo and threw him in the steamer. "Time to split the beach and head for home, when he comes around he's going to hunt us down," she said as they steamed back up the beach to meet Major.

"Why does he hate me so much?" Milo thought to himself as they steamed up the beach. The sun was settling below the horizon when they met up with Major. Milo's unscheduled adventure had interrupted the boiler prep so they were still low on steam and would not make it to the safety of the tree line before dark. "We'll camp here tonight to re-stoke the boilers," Milo directed. "Let's build a fire for fresh hot embers but put it out before we turn in. Uno doesn't prowl at night but no sense taking the chance, he might be just mad enough to start. We'll head home at sunrise."

Back where they left him the big bruised Eagle was still on his back staring at the night's young stars. His head had cleared and his body was sore but not broken. The soft sandy beach had cushioned his abrupt landing well enough to avoid damage to anything other than his pride.

"I had him," he thought to himself. "He was right there!" Springing to his feet he swore to himself, "tomorrow will be the day, yes, tomorrow will be the day I put an end to that pack rat's pilfering!"

Running up to the big birds side a winded Weasel looked up and said, "did you see that Milo can fly!"

"Shut up," said the angry Eagle as he fell back on his back. "Just shut up and do your job"

"On it," said the Weasel as he faded back into the night

Chapter 6
(Change Is A Com'in)

THE CREW GOT AS FAR down the beach as they could before stopping for the night. The boilers were dry so they had to get them full and reheated before heading for home. They would get an early start before making a beeline for the tree line path that would give them the cover and security to make it home. As they came to a stop Tinker couldn't wait any longer for Milo's report on the flight.

"What was it like, what was it like Milo?" she asked excitedly. "How did it feel to soar to the skies?"

Milo tilted his head and thought for a minute. "Well, when I first took off it was terrifying, and when I got real high it was terrifying, then hitting Uno was confusing and when I started to fall back it got terrifying again and spinning down with Uno on my tail was terrifying so I guess that was pretty much it," he explained. "Completely terrifying with a wee bit of confusion."

Tinker looked at him with joy, slapped him on the back and exclaimed, "Awesome!"

"Whatever," Milo answered, shaking his head. "Once the boilers are topped off and we have enough hot coals let's put out the fire and get a little sleep. No sense leaving a beacon of our position burning all night," he pointed out.

Hunkered in the darkness in a nearby tuft of brush the creepy weasel watched and listened as the crew settled in for the night.

Milo tossed his blanket to the sand. As he stretched one last time before calling it a day, he sensed something in the air. Actually, he smelled something in the air. "Anybody else think it smells a little weasely around here?" he asked the others.

Putting their noses to the breeze they all shook their heads to the affirmative.

"Okay Sleazball if you're planning on an ambush you might want to park it downwind," he shouted. "We know you're out there."

Coming in from the darkness as if he was invited to a party Sleazal announced his intentions.

"Hi guys and gorgeous gal," he said tipping his head towards Tinker who cringed at the compliment from a creep.

"I'm not here to ambush you," Said the sneering weasel. "I'm here to offer you the chance of a lifetime. The opportunity to seize this island for ourselves."

Somewhat confused and very leery the crew looked around at each other and shrugged.

"No thanks, "said Milo," now if you don't mind we have things to do, such as anything except this."

"But we can do it," the insistent weasel went on. "I am Slaysall, conquering is my blood. With your advanced weapons and my conquering skills we can take out that half sighted Eagle and take control of this whole island."

"What are you talking about," asked a befuddled Milo. "Advanced weapons? All we have are pocket knives that we use as tools not weapons. Have you recently hit your head?"

"I know if I were you I'd try to hide it too but I saw you get a direct hit with that bird seeking missile. All we have to do it send it up one more time unmanned with a little more juice and POW the eagle will be history and I'll be in charge, I mean we'll be in charge."

"Yeah, I'm pretty sure I know what you mean," Milo answered.

"That is not a weapon," Tinker angrily jumped in. "I don't make weapons, but I'm tempted to make one with your name on it!"

"Just get out of here Sleazball," Milo added. "Except for one too many weasels we think this island is great the way it is.

"Okay but that big dumb bird hates you cleaning his beaches, so you better get him before he gets you," pitched the weasel as he scurried back to the darkness.

"Well, that was twenty minutes of our lives we'll never get back," Milo said shaking his head. "Let's hit the sack the sun won't come up any later."

Stars still glowed in the clear darkness above as Milo and the crew woke early and prepped to head home. Only near the horizon did the pitch-black sky blend to a deep blue as the first rays of sunlight flowed over Earth's edge. They knew once they made it back to the tree-lined path they'd be safe the rest of the way home. The path had been here over a century and was the point of the Founders first foray inland. As they founded the village the original collectors would forge on foot and drag whatever they found back by hand which slowly formed a clear lane through the brush. As time went by they progressed to carts and eventually Tinker's steam machines which packed the ground and cleared the sides to form the highway home it was today.

"Okay guys let's get this load back to the village," Milo said through a yawn. "There will be plenty of daylight before we make it to the tree line so hopefully Uno will sleep in. If he does show up you keep going and I'll break off to pull him away. He'll follow me."

"He always goes for me," he thought to himself.

It was slow going for the fully loaded treader but by daybreak they had made it to the line of dunes. You would think a century of crossing these sandy hills would have worn a straight path through to the tree line but every day the ocean breeze shifts the salty sand filling in any disturbance made the day before. Every time the crew crossed the shifting grainy hills it was a whole new world. Deuce went ahead to set the trail with Major and Tinker following in the treader, Milo in the rear would stop from time to time on top of a dune to scout for the angry eagle he sensed was back on the prowl. Banging across the bumpy dunes was a rough ride so halfway to the tree line they stopped in a crevice at the base of some dunes to stretch their legs and tighten down the cargo.

"We're making good time," said Milo leaning way back to stretch his spine. "Get plenty of water in you cause I think this should be our last rest stop."

"Yeah, old man sun is brutal today," added Deuce, "I catch all its rays being on the bike so this shade feels great. I hope that cloud sticks around."

"What cloud?" Milo questioned. "I haven't seen a cloud all day." Looking around they all realized that the refreshing shade cloud cooling Deuce was circling around them and had the definite shape of spread wings.

"UNO!" they all screamed as they scrambled back to the steam machines.

"Keep heading for the trees," Milo yelled to the crew. "Stay low as long as you can, I'll cruise the peaks to draw him away."

"Be Careful Milo!" Tinker yelled back, "Keep your steam mean!"

Milo shot to the top of the dune heading back towards the beach to draw Uno away from the crew. Looking into the bright sun he still couldn't make out the big eagle, but a quick glance back revealed the angry bird's shadow was no longer circling, it was now without doubt heading his way. It worked, Uno had followed as expected so it was now mano y mano, all he had to do was evade him long enough for the crew to get to safety and then hopefully get himself there too.

He stayed on top of the dune heading back towards the beach to draw his hunter as far away from the tree line as possible. Sensing the big bird getting closer he spun the steamer to the left shooting down the side of the dune into the safer low crevice. Uno was trying to hide in the glare of the sun so Milo knew he had to get him going north or south to get a solid visual of his attacker. "There you are" Milo thought to himself as he spotted Uno still pretty high up but coming in fast. Pushing to the max atop the ridge he knew he'd have to get low soon or Uno would just pick him off.

"Three, two, one," he thought to himself before yanking a hard left to head to the base of the dunes reversing course as he did. After a short sprint in the opposite direction, he fishtailed the steamer into a one eighty to set up a jump to the next dune. "Okay Mister Eagle let's see where you are," he thought to himself as he pushed steam to gain the speed he needed. Judging his velocity and the height of the dune he pulled into the slope, raced up the side and left the ground. Once airborne everything slowed down as he scanned the skies around him. To the left was the beach, the ocean waves and old Sleazel slinking around. Straight ahead more dunes and to his right in the distance he could see the team making it safely to the tree-line yet in between him and them and much closer to him was Uno swooping by in the opposite direction.

Since he was on the big bird's blind side Milo could tell Uno didn't see him gliding by at first but something, a slight sound or tiny wisp of air, compelled him to turn his head in Milo's direction and a sinister sneer spread across his beak. "Oh boy," thought Milo as he came back to ground on the opposite dune. The landing was rougher than he expected but fortunately he kept his steam. The load he was carrying from the beach and Tinker's crazy flying cylinder were weighing him down, but he had no time to jettison them now. "Just have to try to compensate for the extra load," he thought. Now that he knew the crew was safe in the trees, he could concentrate on getting himself over there. If he took a direct shot at the tree line Uno would easily pick him off so it was time for the ole zig zag. Uno could strike hard and quick from a linear dive but quick changes in direction give him problems.

Milo pushed the steamer to full speed before heading up the dune side. Halfway up he yanked hard to the right and then back to the left at the peak. He had to stay grounded at this point since he couldn't maneuver if he took to the air. Zig zagging up and down the sides of the sandy hills he would make a short straight burst at the bottom of the swells to keep him moving towards the trees. Looking over his shoulder he could see Uno had gained altitude to keep him in his sight. As Milo tacked the steamer into the next dune, he knew Uno would strike soon. He would probably try to get him near the top of a ridge, so the cagey collector zigged or zagged right below the top of a dune and again when he was over the top. As expected, Uno came in hard as Milo neared the peak of the next dune. It was a silent attack as he streaked in from the sky, but Milo jerked to the right just in time. Uno's tail feathers had actually brushed the side of the steamer, but the angry eagle's claws only grabbed sand.

"Close one," Milo thought as he shot back down to the base of the dune. He knew he wasn't out of the woods yet, or in this case into the woods. Without doubt Uno was banking back for another strike. It would take a little time for him to come around and hone back in on his position so Milo decided to stay low as long as he could while charging for the trees. Eventually the low ground runs out as the dunes blend together so he'd have to surface to the top a few more times before finding safety amongst the dense lower foliage in the trees.

"He almost got him!" screamed Tinker from a branch she had scaled to keep an eye on Milo's progress. "We need to help him," she said as she scaled down from her perch. Without another word she jumped on Deuce's cycle, revved up the steam and shot back into the dunes.

"Hey that's my....," a confused Deuce tried to get out as she sped off. "I didn't know she could ride that thing," he said looking back at Major.

"She built it goofball; wouldn't you figure she test drove it a few times," Major responded. "Come on, we're not letting her go alone," he said while easing the treader out of the safety of the trees. Deuce climbed into the passenger seat, folded his arms in frustration at the treaders lack of speed, looked at Major with chagrin and mumbled, "we'll probably die of old age before this gets us there."

Reaching the end of the gully Milo had no choice but to start the zig zag back up. Not knowing which direction the next attack would come from all he could do is stay in motion and keep his eyes in the skies. Reaching the peak he pegged the steamer left to start the downward run. Gaining slope speed he cranked it right to start the zag when the bottom fell out. An empty pocket gave out under the back of the steamer lifting the front end slowing him to a crawl. "Bogged it," he thought to himself as he bounced forward trying to get the front end down. He was still sliding downhill with the sand but much too slow to evade Uno. Right on cue the menacing eagle showed dead ahead screaming towards him in a full speed assault. "Come on, come on," Milo said, trying to muscle the front end down. Uno was closing fast, and Milo knew he'd be on him in seconds, he could tell the steamer wasn't going to grab solid in time so he decided to duck and cover. Uno was ground level with talons out and only one dune away so Milo prepped to hit the floor but what was that sound overhead. Looking up he saw the bottom of Deuce's cycle and heard Tinker screaming "Mean Steam!" as she sailed inches above his head in a straight on assault of the attacking Sea Eagle.

Having no desire to collide with a steam filled hunk of flying metal Uno pulled out of his dive banking swiftly to the right. Looking back in frustration he could see Milo working to get his steamer back in motion so he knew the day would only offer him one more shot. "Third times a charm," he thought while plotting his final assault.

"Whooooooo Hoooooooooo," Milo screamed as the steamer cranked back up to speed. Glancing towards Tinker he screamed her praise, "Tinker you are a warrior!" All memories of his near-death flight strapped to her bird seeking missile were long gone. If she hadn't shown up as big as she just did Milo knew he'd be cruising the skies in Uno's clutches right now.

"Shut up and drive," she yelled back flashing a big smile. As glad as she was to have made it in time, she knew they weren't safe yet. They had two more dunes to get over before finding the low seam that would steer them to the fern covered sanctuary of the tree line. Once there they could celebrate, exposed on the dunes was still focus time.

Milo had the steamer topped back out. No more zig zags, Uno had to regroup and circle back so he was confident he had the time needed to make the trees. Knowing the path to the tree-line trail was just over the next dune he decided the quickest way there was in the air so he cranked the steam to the mean and hit the sandy ramp of the next to last dune at full speed with his sight set on the downhill slope of the next dune over. Leaving clean he knew the steamer had plenty of air and would sail the gap with ease, until he heard a strange flutter.

"Mean Ste..." he started to yell milli-seconds before the sound. Quickly glancing back, he could see the chute from the sky screamer tangled in the load from the beach trying to grab air. Before he could process a thought, the chute popped open full of air killing his momentum and steering the steamer down into a head on collision with the top of the last dune. As the front of the steamer dipped Milo didn't, leaving him flailing in the air above his mean machine, a helpless witness as it rammed the side of the dune. End over end it rolled plowing into the sandy slope of the next dune, scattering the beach load as it tumbled. Milo belly flopped into the side of the dune, spread eagle, half buried he lay motionless. The banged-up steamer lay next to him, bottom side up hissing as the remaining steam poured from the damaged boiler.

Tinker roared in on the cycle, ran over to Milo turning him over out of the sand. "Milo are you okay?" she said with concern as she brushed the sand from his face.

"I think so," he replied in a daze while spitting out a mouthful of sand.

"Are you sure, are you sure you're okay?" she asked.

Taking a moment to answer as he checked to make sure all the body parts were working, he looked at her with a smile and said, "Yeah, yeah I'm good."

Convinced he was fine, Tinker's expression quickly changed from concern to anger. Bopping him on the back of the head she let out a scream "LOOK WHAT YOU DID TO THE STEAMER!"

"What I did?" Milo answered surprised at her sudden outrage.

"Yes you," she came back! "You were the only one in it!"

"It was the chute from your crazy flying tube that brought me down," Milo snapped back.

Pulling up to the top of the dune overlooking the crash scene, Major and Deuce are surprised and confused to see Milo and Tinker in a heated exchange. Knowing this was not a great time for a squabble Major tries to get their attention. "Hey...hey."

Paying no attention Tinker stays in Milo's face, "You didn't have to make a jump, we had plenty of time to just drive on in, but nooo, you had to show off!"

"Heeey," Major tried again.

"Show off," Milo roared back! "I was just."

"Hey, HEY, HHEEEYYYY," Major forced his way in.

"WHAT!" They both looked up and shouted back at him.

Instead of a reply Major pointed down the way. Following his gesture, they both looked around to see Uno perched at the end of the gully, firmly rooted between them and their tree-line escape.

"Eeww that's a problem," Milo stated the obvious.

"Ya think," said Major.

"Okay there's only one of him so same drill as earlier," Milo directed.

"Eehh maybe not," Deuce said with concern while pointing to a Parrot standing atop the next dune over.

"Uno has a friend," a confused Milo asks?

"Friends," Major pointed out. "Many friends."

Birds of all kinds started landing around them. Loons, Terns, Pelicans, Albatross, Gulls every type of bird that lived on the island surrounded their position, cutting off any possible path of escape.

"Maybe this is some mass migration thing and they're not with him," a hopeful Milo suggested.

"They're sure looking at us like they're with him," Tinker added as every bird starred in their direction with piercing eyes.

Uno had not moved towards them. He stood tall, stoic, confident and content that he finally had Milo signed, sealed and delivered.

"Hey Un, throwing a party?" an obviously nervous Milo quipped.

"Yes, Milo I am," he replied with a sinister sneer. "It's a going away party and you are the guest of honor." He found pleasure in the fearful expressions on their faces, until it suddenly changed. Instead of fear they all cocked their heads to the side and looked somewhat confused. "Why do they look so befuddled," he thought before hearing a strange sound approaching from behind. A quick glance back revealed the swaying fat underbelly of a quickly descending Albatross coming right at his head.

"Scuse me, scuse me, coming through," yelled a winded Albert Ross as Uno hit the dirt. Albert did nothing to improve upon the ungraceful reputation of his species as he came in like a sack of spuds, swaying back and forth he bounced and rolled a few times before sprawling on his back in front of his mean steam rat buddies.

"Hey guys, whatcha doing?" he asked as if he had just strolled up on a sunny beach that wasn't surrounded by an angry feathered army.

"Hey Albert," greeted Milo, "good seeing you again but it's really not a great time to be dropping in."

"Really?" Albert replied, "why's that?"

"TROSS!" bellowed a no longer stoic Uno lunging two steps closer. As if on cue every one of the surrounding birds also stepped forward in an uncomfortable display of two step unity.

"That's why," Milo pointed out as Albert struggled to his feet brushing off the sand.

"I told you to mind your own business, Tross," the obviously agitated Sea Eagle grumbled. "This is none of your concern and believe me you don't want it to be! Now turn around, get your clumsy tail end in the air and don't look back cause I don't want to go through you to get to them."

"Now, now there's need for any bird on bird violence or any violence for that matter," Albert calmly replied. "You see sir I have a debt of gratitude to repay these young scavengers for saving me from a precarious predicament I found myself in after being deposited on your shores by the recent glorious gale."

Two steps forward came the Eagle, two steps forward came the mob, now joined by a sneering weasel.

"Though saving me from a lifeless inert tangle of net may not be quite the same as what we have here, I still feel compelled to intervene on their behalf," Albert offered, not as calm as before. "It's true I've only known Milo, Tinker, Major and Deuce a brief moment in time. I have no doubt they are decent at heart and except for perhaps some youthful transgressions offer no ill will or malice towards any of you."

"They're thieves!" Uno bellowed.

Two steps forward, two steps forward.

"Now Mr. Uno," Albert started to say.

"THAT'S NOT MY NAME!" The very agitated Eagle shouted. "HE CALLS ME THAT!" pointing to Milo, "My name is Ulysses."

"Well sir that's a Grant name," Albert joked, trying unsuccessfully to break the tension. "Get it Grant, grand?" he clarified while scanning the crowd when suddenly it hit him why Ulysses would be angry at the nickname Milo gave him.

Turning to the now contrite pack leader, "Making fun of a man's handicap Milo?" Albert said with disappointment for all to hear. "Mr. Ulysses, maybe you should eat him."

"Wait what," a stunned Milo whispers.

"Eat him, I don't want to eat him, that's gross." responded the disgusted bird. "I don't even want to kill him. To be honest I'm not sure what I was going to do with him, but I'll do whatever it takes to get them to stop stealing."

Two steps. Two steps.

Ulysses and his feathered friends were now uncomfortably close. Any thoughts of escape were pointless, there were far too many to fight and too close together to run through.

"Stealing?" Albert asked. "By cleaning the beach? From what I can tell they're just doing their job and doing it very well I might add. Your beaches are immaculate, some of the cleanest I've ever seen."

"That's my point," countered Ulysses. They steal everything off the beach before we can get what we need to build our nests. Twigs, moss, twine, net scraps cleared from the beach before we can get any and all they leave are those awful cold crunchy clear bottles. Have you ever tried to sleep in a nest made of those? It's cold, it pops and cracks with every move."

"Can't say that I have, but it sounds terrible." Albert responded sympathetically.

"I haven't had a decent night's sleep since she invented those awful contraptions!" responded the Eagle pointing to Tinker and the steam machines.

"But I wasn't trying to..." Tinker tried to explain before being cut off.

"It's true," interrupted a motherly Gull. It's so hard to raise my babies in a clear hard nest. It's slippery and cold, I have to stay with them all the time to keep them warm. If Ulysses wasn't bringing us food we'd starve to death."

"That's right," added an elderly gray Parrot. "My arthritis was crippling me in that cold, hard, noisy nest. Thank goodness for Ulysses there, he flew to another island to get me some moss for padding and warmth.

"Commendable," an impressed Albert said, nodding to the big Eagle.

"It hasn't always been like this," added an elderly Tern. "When they were collecting by hand or using push carts there would always be enough for everyone. But with those machines they clear the beach so fast and leave nothing for us to use."

"But it's just progress," Tinker defended, upset that she may have hurt others. "I was just trying to make things better and life easier."

"I'm afraid progress isn't a cure all Tinker," Alfred explained. "Sometimes innovation is just trading one problem for another. For example, those clear bottles everyone's complaining about are made of something called plastic. It was a great new product, lighter than glass, easier to make and unbreakable, it solved a lot of problems, so everyone started using it. Problem is it lasts forever so now those bottles are floating in every sea and washing up on every beach. One problem solved, another created."

Milo had heard enough. He knew the only way to resolve this was to go face to face with the big bird. Forsaking the security of Albert's big body, he slowly walked straight up to Ulysses and stood right in front of him.

"Milo no," Tinker cried.

"He'll be okay," Albert reassured her.

Looking up into the giant birds piercing glare Milo's knees wobbled some as he realized how huge his nemesis actually was. This was the first time they had actually stood front to front, it was not comforting. Gathering all the courage he could muster Milo looked straight into that glare and said what he knew needed to be said.

"Mr. Ulysses, we owe you an apology, we owe all of you an apology," he said, gesturing to the surrounding flock.

The crowd murmured in agreement, but Ulysses was not convinced. "You owe us more than that," he sternly stated.

"Yes sir, we do," Milo continued. "There is a saying in our village that if you want good neighbors, you must first be one. We haven't lived up to that. We were just trying to do our job and provide for our colony but in doing so we deprived you, our neighbors."

"Yes, you have Milo," lectured Ulysses, but saying you're sorry does not resolve the issue."

"No sir but if you'll agree to it, we'd like to try and make it up to you. My crew and I will continue to sweep the beaches clean but when we're done we'll leave most of the nest building materials stacked near the dunes for all of you to use. We'll keep the bigger chunks of wood, anything metal and a little bit of net for the village but twigs, seaweed and most of the net scrapes will be left behind in a neat stack for all of you."

Ulysses scanned the surrounding crowd and could see they were all bobbing their heads in approval. "Okay Milo it's a deal," he said, "but if you don't follow through, I will swallow you."

Milo gulped, "I thought you didn't want to eat me," he replied.

"I don't," chuckled Ulysses, "but it rhymed."

"Hey that was good," Milo grinned as he turned back to the crew, "he made a joke, Uno made a...I mean Mr. Ulysses made a joke."

Pleased to find the big bad Eagle not only had a heart but also a sense of humor he knew there was no time like the present to come through on his promise.

"We start today," he declared. "Major dump that load and let our neighbors take whatever they want."

"You got it!" Major answered as he and Deuce released the bonds holding the load to the trailer allowing the bounty of material to hit the ground to be shared with the gleeful feathered crowd.

Tinker picked up a wad of moss and carried it to the Mother Gull. "I'm sorry mam, I just wanted to make the boys more efficient. I'm so sorry," she explained as a tear fell from her eye.

"It's okay dear you meant no harm and now your machines will provide for us all," consoled Mother Gull. "You're an amazing young lady and I hope my daughters grow up to be as resourceful and driven as you."

Albert, Milo and Ulysses watched from the side of the dune as Deuce, Major and Tinker assisted the diverse flock in sorting materials they could use to build sturdy comfortable nests. There wouldn't be enough for everyone today but in the weeks to come the crew would provide for all.

"Seeing an opportunity to better his situation Sleazel swooped in to hog as much as he could for his own gain. Grabbing armloads he could he started hogging most of the bounty for himself.

Not noticing the weasel being a weasel Ulysses turned to Albert. "Since this seems to be an apology party, I guess I owe you one Ross," Ulysses admitted." I may have overreacted some and if you hadn't intervened this may not have ended as well. If you decide to stick around awhile you are more than welcome here."

"I guess there's an apology in there somewhere," Albert replied winking at Milo. "Thank you for the invitation but I'm a wandering soul destined to roam so I can't see me dropping anchor just yet, but ya know it would be nice to have a place to come home to so I have a feeling I'll be back."

"All right!" Milo yelled, happy to have his new friend around at times. Turning to Ulysses Milo looked up and asked, "so big guy you and me are good now right, hatchet buried, hostilities ceased, peace on earth and goodwill towards me?"

Looking down with a snide grin Ulysses replied, "we're good for now runt but if you ever fly into my air space and hit me in the butt with a rocket again all bets are off."

"Oh, I missed that," Albert said with gusto, "you need to fill me in on that Milo."

"Oh just one of Tinkers toys that shot me in the air and almost killed me and Mr. Ulysses here," Milo told him. "By the way Big Guy that furry sidekick of yours approached us about using it to take you out for good so he could take over this place."

"WHAT!" The big bird roared as his expression jumped from serene to intense anger in a second. Turning to find the conniving weasel he spots him grabbing some nesting material from the Mother Gull. "Gotta go," he grunted. Eyes glowing with fury he shot into the air effortlessly clearing the distance between him and the weasel in a fraction of a second, he grabbed him in his talons and glided up and over the tree.

"Heyyyyyyy!" is all you could hear from the startled weasel as they screamed out towards the sea.

"Dang, think he's going to kill him?" Albert asked.

"Nah he's probably just going to take him back to where he came from," Milo answered.

"Probably?" Albert questioned.

"Yeah, I mean he can be tough, but he wouldn't go that far." Milo says with a bit less conviction.

"Yeah, probably not," agreed the Albatross.

"Maybe I shouldn't have mentioned that last part," Milo sheepishly admits.

"You knew what you were doing," Albert chuckled back at him."

Milo just smiled.

The End
{For Now}

Don't miss out!

Visit the website below and you can sign up to receive emails whenever J. H. Williams publishes a new book. There's no charge and no obligation.

https://books2read.com/r/B-A-XXHV-ZOSBC

BOOKS 2 READ

Connecting independent readers to independent writers.